This book is dedicated to

Morton Park

With all of her beauty and splendor, it will always be home to me and I will always find peace and solitude in your arms. I am thankful for all the wonderful memories that were built there and have a special fondness for those still there, in person and spirit, who keep its integrity and grandeur.

To John

Enjoy my fav. story!

Denise Tobin

Secrets in the Woods

Chapter 1

Welcome to Morton Park

Morton Park is a beautiful town forest located a mile west of Plymouth Bay. The property is owned by a town of the same name and comprises approximately 200 acres of beautiful forest surrounding a little pond, appropriately named Little Pond. The body of water itself is the deepest in the entire county despite its shore having the smallest circumference. This little natural pool covers a total of only 43 acres but its average depth is, surprisingly, 19 feet with one area plunging even further to a murky 51 feet below its glassy surface.

The woods are full of pine and oak, deer and wild turkeys. The ground is covered by a thick blanket of pine needles with moss and wildflowers scattered throughout. And, in the spring, patches of lady slippers can be found poking through. There's a dirt road at the entrance to the park on the north side that runs down to the pond. It circles around the water to a secondary entrance on the east side.

On the opposite side, another dirt road darts in closer to the pond. It's a dead end lane named Burgess Road. There are six houses lining this little street, three on each side, and those fortunate families who reside there enjoy the luxury of a quiet and peaceful way of life, until summer arrives.

From Memorial Day to Labor Day, the town opens the two public beaches on Little Pond. One is on the north side, at the bottom of the entrance road and a smaller beach located on the east side. Both are popular spots for families to picnic and swim. There are always lots of people flocking there on the weekends enjoying the pond, having cookouts and playing horseshoes. The weekdays are filled more with mothers bringing their children to swimming lessons and trying to escape the summer heat with a dip in the cool water.

There, originally, were just two houses on Burgess Road. Old man Raggazini's at the far end on the pond side and Rose and Owen Callahan's across from Ken Raggazini's on a wooded lot set back from the street. The Callahan's are retired, including Owen's service as a former town selectman. The two never did have children but they do have a black Lab named Gibby who is more like a son to them than a pet.

Ken Raggazini is a strange fellow. He's what one might call "shell shocked". He was a Colonel in the Army Air Corps during World War II and a widower at a young age. He spends most days tinkering in his garage on a work bench and most evenings wandering the woods surrounding the neighborhood alone. What waking moments he has left place him in his garden, always smoking Marlboros and always drinking Miller High Life. He typically keeps to himself and doesn't talk much with his neighbors, especially the *new three*. The three young families with children, who moved in within the past ten years, are viewed by Ken as "the new three." He has an occasional visit from an old Air Force buddy who lives down on the Cape in Hyannis. They have been known to throw a few beers back in Ken's garage or down at the Plymouth VFW.

The third house in the neighborhood is the first house on the wooded side, owned by Phyllis. Dear old Phyllis. Phyllis is 102 if she is a day. She wears a housecoat all summer and is more than a bit eccentric. She loves the summertime when people crowd the beach. Mostly because she takes her evening walks to the waterside and collects all the bottles and beer cans and brings them home to drink the leftover contents. She finds quite a bit of whiskey. Apparently it's the drink of choice for a lot of townspeople celebrating on their days' off from the mill. And Phyllis is not fussy. Scotch, Bourbon, Vodka, they all suit her. Everyone knows not to accept a drink from her at home.

The *new three* are the new houses built within the last ten years. They are the first two on the pond side and the middle house on the wooded side. They all house young couples with school aged children. The middle house on the wooded side belongs to Laura and Bobby Stevens and is commonly known as the party house. Bobby's a top ad executive at a widely respected Boston advertising agency. He commutes to his office every day in his 1968 black Cadillac. Laura stays at home with the children and usually entertains other ladies in her circle at her house each Monday for a standing card game. The weekends are another thing altogether. The Stevens' have a basement bar that hosts a party on Saturday nights for neighbors and other friends to gather.

The first two houses on the pond side are occupied by Marie and Paul Anderson and

Nanette and Peter Damon. They each have two school aged boys. Both houses are set at the end of fairly long driveways descending down through some woods to the pond. They are twin houses built by the same builder. Each one is a three bedroom standard Cape style home with wood shingles and a dock behind the house. The three younger couples have become close and enjoy their Saturday night parties. Parties that occasionally get cut short when Ken calls the cops for "excessive noise."

Despite the quirks, things in the neighborhood were going pretty well until the summer of 1968. That's when strange things started to happen…*very* strange.

Chapter 2

Now That's a Party

"Bobby, did you get enough ice at the store?" yelled Laura down the basement stairs as she heard Bob entering through the bulkhead out back. "Sure did! We won't run out this week for sure!" The Stevens' basement was finished with a completely stocked bar, several couches and a shag orange rug in the center. And, unusual for the neighborhood, they even had a second TV down there to get sports games on Sundays.

In the corner was a new hi-fi stereo with a shelf above it full of records. It was a Fisher, top of the line. There were plastic patio lantern lights strung across the ceiling and the bar was complete with a dancing hula girl and bobbing ostriches. The back of the bar had a Miller High Life sign that actually lit up.

"Laura, everyone should be here at seven. I invited some friends from the lodge this week so you'd better make some extra food."

"You know me," Laura replied, "I always have extra everything." She walked down the stairs in a new purple mini skirt with a low cut white sheer top and white sandals. As usual, she had spent the day in rollers, preparing her clothes and face for company. "How do I look?" she asked.

"Great honey, maybe a little more make up, I can start to see your age a bit," he said as he briefly looked up from stocking the fridge.

"Sure thing Bobby," she said and ran back upstairs to her vanity where she, nervously, primped and puffed her face some more. She was always so eager to please her husband. It seemed to be more difficult each year to keep his attentions on her.

The Stevens kids were fed early and sent over to the babysitter at the Anderson's house for a sleepover as was the Saturday night custom. By seven, the neighbors started to arrive along with a few couples from the lodge. The music was loud and, with the bulkhead and windows open, the sound travelled across the pond.

The Callahan's were out on their back porch having their Saturday night martinis. The party next door flowed into their back yard as it usually did. Bobby called over "Come join us for a drink."

"No thanks, Bobby, you kids enjoy," responded Owen as he lifted his glass in the motion of a toast.

Ken could be seen working in his lit up garage down the hill, always shaking his head and mumbling to himself. It was getting past nine and almost time for his nightly rounds. He did not condone parties, drinking or all of the philandering he had been witnessing each week. His disdain for how the neighborhood was changing had been growing more and more each year.

Back at the party, the booze was flowing and the laughter and music seemed to be growing. Bobby was paying exceptional attention to Nanette as he seemed to be doing as of late. She'd recently dyed her hair a blazing red and it was becoming. Her husband Peter paid no mind as the more he drank the less interested he was in anything except talking sports. He was the manager downtown at the Woolworths. If you came in for lunch at the counter he would give you a play-by-play of last night's game, whatever the sport.

Laura tried to get Bobby's attention and walked past him while he was in deep conversation with Nanette. She ran her fingers through his hair. "Nanette, doesn't my husband have the lushest head of hair you've ever seen on a man? He just loves when I do this. Don't you dear?" she said.

Bobby turned his attention to Laura for a moment. "Honey, go and get me a new scotch and water, will you? Nanette what can she get you?"

"I'll have a martini if it's not too much trouble, Laura," she said.

"Not at all," Laura responded, a little too sweetly to be genuine, as she went behind the bar to make the two cocktails with a little twist of resentment.

The party continued until, once again, Ken called the cops at one in the morning. As usual, Sgt. Andy Colman showed up. He was a friend of just about everyone in town and one of the twenty eight officers on the town's small police department. He grew up in town and had the most seniority of anyone on the department. He lived a few miles away in North Plymouth and it had turned into a bit of a habit on his way home on Saturday nights to go by the Stevens house and shepherd all the party goers back to their own homes.

"OK folks, you know the drill," would be the call to go home. They always tried to get him to join the party but he managed, instead, to get them all headed out and on their way every week.

This week was the same for all except Peter Damon who was passed out on one of the couches.

"Just leave him there," said Bobby. "Come on Nanette, I'll walk you across the street."

"Oh don't bother," said the Andersons almost in unison. "We're going that way. We'll take her."

Chapter Three

Damn Dog!

"Knock, knock it's me, Marie. Kids, where is your mother?" Marie asked as she opened the Damon's back screen door.

"Hi Marie, come on in. I'm in the bedroom. You kids get outside and play," yelled Nanette from her room.

As Marie walked in, she could see Nanette admiring her new swim suit. Holding it up on a hanger, she turned to Marie and said "Isn't it the top of the line? I can't wait to wear it." It was a baby blue bikini covered with green turtles.

"Oh Nanette, Peter is going to love you in that little number."

"Hmmm I guess," Nanette replied, "but I got it for myself." She pulled the suit against her body and looked in the mirror. "I thought the blue would match my eyes."

Just then they heard the children screaming and crying outside. "Oh, for goodness sake, who do you suppose started it this time?" Nanette laughed as she carefully placed her new suit on the bed and headed outside, with Marie close behind.

As they reached the yard, they could see the kids were terribly upset and were hollering for their mom. Ken had their little poodle, Tuppy, by the scruff of his neck and was walking him back into their yard. All the children in the neighborhood were afraid of old man Raggazini so any interaction with him was cause for complete panic and chaos.

"WHAT ON EARTH ARE YOU *DOING*, KEN?!" shouted Nanette.

"I'm returning your dog. He's been digging up my tomatoes …AGAIN!" said Ken as he dropped the dog in Nanette's backyard. "There's a leash law in this town."

"Ken, I swear you are outrageous! Now look what you've done. I have a pile of screaming kids and a terrified little puppy," Nanette blurted out, barely able to contain herself.

"Kids get back in the house and take the dog. Ken, you are a vile old man," she shouted as she spun to follow her children through the back door.

"You listen up, Missy. Keep that dog off my property or you won't *have* a dog anymore,"

Ken hollered after her as he headed for his own home.

"Oh Ken, don't you have someone else to bother," she retorted from the safety of the screened door. Nanette was always compelled to get the last word. She turned to Marie as they gathered the kids, "I swear there is something creepy about that man. He's always lurking around and he stares at me funny."

Marie chuckled, "It could be your short shorts." They laughed, hugged the kids and then suddenly realized the commotion had made them three minutes late for their favorite soap opera. As was their daily routine, they rushed to the living room and breathlessly turned on the television.

Later, that evening Nanette just happened to be at her mailbox in her new bikini at 5:50 pm, which also just happened to be the same time that Bobby arrived home each evening from his job in Boston.

As he slowly pulled into his driveway, Bobby simply could not keep his eyes off of her. He parked and walked down to his own mailbox across the street from his house which was next to Nanette's. "That's quite the suit!" he said. "With all those turtles you should walk it on down to Turtle Cove for a swim."

"Bobby you must be reading my mind," she said seductively. "I was just headed that way. This July heat is too much for me. Besides you never know who you might run into down there." She winked and walked back to her house.

Turtle Cove is located on the southwest side of the pond. It's a short walk through the woods from the houses and known as a private little nook for couples looking to get away.

Bobby ran into his house and threw on his swim trunks. "Laura, when's dinner? It's hot as hell in here."

Laura came from the kitchen saying, "I made a roast. That's why the house is so hot. Why are you wearing your swimming trunks?"

"I've gotta go take a dip and cool down," he said as he breezed past her.

"Well dinner is in an hour. Don't be late," she called after him but Bobby was already out the door. She stared at him through the screen as he ran down through the back woods until he was consumed by the trees and then she just kept on staring out at the thickening woods, lost in thought. The kids running through the house yanked her sharply back from her daydreams with a jolt that made her shudder for a moment as if waking suddenly from a deep sleep.

Ken was out for his after dinner walk in the woods and could hear voices coming from the cove just south of his property. As he walked further, he came across a blue bikini with green turtles hanging on a branch. He looked down the hill into Turtle Cove and could see two people, with familiar faces, swimming. . . naked. Interesting he thought, but not surprising, as he turned and walked back toward his house.

Chapter 4

Where is that Dog?

It was late Monday afternoon and the ladies in the neighborhood were just finishing up their card game at Laura's house. Laura came from the kitchen with a small birthday cake with one pink candle in the center. "Happy birthday Marie!" Laura sang out.

 "Oh, I am going to simply spoil my appetite for dinner but you know I will have a big piece of that cake. Thank you gals so much," said Marie.

"Laura, do you have any more of your famous rum & iced tea to wash this cake down with?" asked Nanette.

"Yes, let me get refills," Laura replied. Just then the phone rang. "Oh hello Carol, no, no, no, OK," she spoke into the phone and then hung up. She rolled her eyes and said "That was Bobby's secretary Carol…*again*. She has all day with him but seems to call here several times a week lately for some urgent question. She is so obvious with her school girl crush."

"Well," said Marie, "that's what happens when you marry tall dark and handsome."

They all laughed.

As Laura went back to the kitchen she heard Marie say "Oh my, I almost forgot! Look, girls, at the beautiful necklace Paul gave me for my birthday. It's Irish and called a

Claddagh. That's a real emerald in the center," she said as her face beamed.

Marie turned to Nanette and asked "Did the kids find your dog today?"

"Who knows?"

"That dog is always missing," Laura yelled from the kitchen, "he's probably under the bed like last time."

Rose, who was typically very quiet, noted how lovely the necklace was but said she had to excuse herself and get home as she always had Owen's dinner prepared and ready for him promptly each and every night. As she was leaving, the other ladies gathered their things and finished their drinks.

It was already past 5:45 so Marie and Nanette started to head home to get their own dinners ready as well. As they were leaving, Bobby's car was coming up the road. He passed Phyllis walking up to the Anderson's house carrying their dog, Tuppy, in her arms.

As Phyllis got to the Anderson's and Damon's driveways, everyone's attention went to her. They could see she was crying and Tuppy was limp in the arms. Nanette ran towards her and started screaming as she got closer to Phyllis. She could see that the little dog was covered in blood. Bobby ran down his driveway and, as Nanette dramatically dropped to her knees, he knelt beside her to comfort her.

Laura and Marie came running and helped Phyllis with the dog. Paul was just arriving home as well. He rushed to the growing crowd and Rose and Owen came out of their home as well. Ken stood a distance away and watched it all from his driveway.

Paul took the dog from the ladies and he and Marie brought Tuppy to their yard. "I'll help Peter bury him tonight," he said grimly.

Bobby helped Nanette up and was walking her back towards her driveway just as she saw Ken standing in his driveway watching them.

"KEN! YOU *MURDERED* HIM!" she screamed.

Bobby was holding her by her shoulders. "Nanette, stop that. That's a ridiculous thing to say."

"No," she cried out, "he *hated* that dog! I *know* he did it."

Ken shook his head, looked at the ground and turned to walk home. "Nanette, don't worry about anything," Bobby said as softly as he could. "Paul and Peter will take care of the dog tonight."

She turned to Bobby and said. "Don't you think it's about time we tell Peter and Laura about us?"

"NO!" he blurted, trying desperately to keep his voice down. "You're acting emotional and crazy. You need to settle down. I am *not* leaving my wife and children. Maybe we should cool things a little."

Nanette's crying only grew worse as she begged him not to shut her out. "No Nanette," he said apologetically, "it's over. We really did let things go too far and it's time to stop. You're getting too emotional. Now go on inside and try to calm down." She turned and ran into the house. The entire neighborhood could hear her slamming things around and yelling at the kids.

Later that evening, Paul was out back digging a hole, awaiting Peter's return home from work at the Woolworths, when they would bury the dog together. As he dug, Marie came back outside. "She sounds really upset. She's still in the house crying."

"You know, Marie, that strikes me strange because she never hid her feelings of disdain for that dog," said Paul. "I think she really must believe Ken had something to do with it. She's in there cursing "*that man*" and slamming things around."

"Let's just hope she settles down before Peter gets home," added Marie. "That poor man has had his hands full with her for years. Remember a couple years ago when she had that affair with the butcher down at Perry's Meat?"

"Ohhh boy, yeah . . . what a scandal that was!" Paul remembered. "You know they would meet down in Cordage Park right in the middle of the day. It's a wonder they weren't caught sooner. Anyway, can you get an old blanket that we can use to wrap this little guy in to keep the dirt off of him?"

"Sure, Paul, I'll get one."

Chapter 5

New Tupperware

Detective Andy Colman was spending the day sitting at his brand new desk, in the new police station on Russell Street, catching up on paperwork. The Plymouth Police Department had been growing and, now, with its roster up to 28 patrolmen, along with a handful of management this year, they moved into number 25 Russell Street. The new station had created some talk in the neighborhood, located just behind the center of downtown Plymouth, since the bars on the cell block windows on the ground floor led some neighbors to think prisoners were being held just a little too close to home. Some of the elderly residents felt the prisoners might try a *"great escape"* and make their way through the neighborhood.

"Call for you, Colman, on line two," hollered the dispatcher.

"Detective Colman here," he answered. "Oh I see, Mrs. Anderson. You don't say. Mmm hmm, you don't say. Oh, you don't say. Hmmm. yes, I will look into it, but without proof there is not a lot I can do for you." He hung up, sighed and shook his head.

The dispatcher leaned back in his chair. "Women . . . huh?"

"Well, some of 'em, at least . . . and their imaginations. I think those new day time soap operas are to blame," he replied. They laughed.

"It seems lately we get more calls about those six little houses up there in the woods than we do for the rest of West Plymouth altogether," the dispatcher groaned.

"I guess you can't pick your neighbors," admitted Coleman as he hunched back over the stack of papers on his desk.

Days passed and it was Monday once more. That meant the ladies were, again, gathering at the Stevens house for cards. Marie was the first to arrive.

"Hello Marie, come in. I'm so glad you came early," said Laura. "I was hoping we could talk in private. I'm not sure if it's my imagination or not but something has been bothering me. Do you think Nanette and Bobby have been getting too close lately?"

"Not at all, Laura. What would make you think such a thing? You know what a big flirt Nanette is, and Bobby as well. I'm sure it's just that."

"I guess you're right," agreed Laura. "Maybe it *is* my imagination. Oh Marie, is that what I think it is?" Laura pointed to the bag in Marie's hand.

"You know it" Marie responded. "The Tupperware order is in. I brought over your new tumblers and bowls. Enjoy them and thanks again for bringing that fantastic dip to the party this weekend."

"Oh Marie, these tumblers are great! I love the colors. We can use them today to serve our Long Island ice teas. I'll give you the blue to match your eyes and, of course, the pink to Rose. And we have to give Nanette the peach color since she's so peachy. I'll mix up a batch of cocktails right now."

The other women arrived and the game began. "Laura, this drink is *strong*," exclaimed Nanette.

"That's funny coming from you," Rose smirked. They all got a good laugh out of that since Nanette was known to throw a few back. Every day.

"By the way, I called the police on Ken a few days ago. I told them he killed my dog," Nanette said with a bit of a triumphant grin. "That will show that mean old man. He's so strange, always roaming around the neighborhood at all hours and he's forever banging away in that garage. It is absolutely annoying."

"Oh my, Nanette," said Rose, "he is harmless! He's just an old 'shell shocked' veteran from World War Two. He keeps to himself. You know he has a difficult time with all the changes in the neighborhood. For years it was just our two houses and, since his wife passed, he's just a shell of his past self."

"I thought it was determined that Tuppy was hit by a car on the road out by the beach," Laura added.

"Well yes, but I'm sure it was Ken," Nanette said with a strange look in her eye. "I think he's doing all sorts of things over at that house. Frankly, he scares me."

"Nanette you're acting crazy. His truck has been jacked up with only three wheels on it all summer," said Marie.

"Don't call me crazy!" Nanette's voice began to elevate. She took another gulp of her drink as she stood up and bellowed, "Peter thinks I *am* crazy and he has me taking all this medicine from Dr. Isaacs for my headaches and it's confusing me." She took another couple of gulps. "Actually my headache is back. I need to go home and lay down." Out she stormed, as she often did after a few drinks . . . like a runaway train.

Well, my, oh my, that was strange," Rose stated as she started to pick up the cards. "I guess our game is cut short today. See you ladies later."

With Marie and Laura alone again, Marie turned to her friend and exclaimed, "That's odd. I guess I'll go check on her."

"Marie, don't bother. I made a big batch of soup yesterday," said Laura. "I'll bring her some later and pick up her kids. They can sleep over here tonight so she can rest. Do you know they have been eating TV dinners and cereal for the past week? It's a shame. She just seems odd since that incident with her dog."

"OK, maybe I'll make her my tuna noodle casserole," said Marie. "You know how she loves that. She's looking so thin. I think she's lost a lot of weight. Maybe *I* should get a dead dog," she joked as she looked out the front picture window towards the Damon's house. Then, quickly returning to the seriousness of the situation, she turned to Laura with a worried look.

"I think she's having a nervous breakdown over that dog," Laura whispered, as if the comment was so inflammatory that she didn't want anyone, including Marie, to actually hear her say it.

"What do you mean, Laura? She hated that dog!"

"Maybe so, but ever since that night she hasn't been the same. That must be the cause," Laura insisted.

Marie gathered her things and headed toward the door. She turned back one last time and said, "Hmm, you're probably right. By the way, let's make this Saturday night's party a great one. Its Labor Day weekend, after all, and it seems like every one of us could use a little cheering up. Let's talk tomorrow and make a plan."

Chapter 6

Saturday Night's

All Right for Parties

Paul and Marie had the babysitter settled at their house with all the kids on the street and were dressed to head over to the Stevens' for what was to be the biggest party of the summer. There were cars already parked on both sides of the street. Except, of course, in front of Ken's house. Everyone knew not to park there. Even Rose and Owen would be there. As they passed Phyllis still outside in her housecoat, they yelled over to her "Aren't you going next door?"

"I sure am. I wouldn't miss it for the world."

Marie whispered to Paul, "She wouldn't miss all the free booze." They laughed behind their warm smiles pointed in her direction. Phyllis was such a quirky old lady.

"You've just gotta love her, don't you?" said Paul.

The music was loud and the basement bar was full. There were people in the yard and the house was crowded. Men were out back playing horseshoes and smoking cigars. Several women filled the kitchen and patio trying, in vain, to figure out where to put all the food. Laughter filled the air and everyone was in great spirits. Even Peter had wandered over from across the street. He had been so drained lately taking care of his sick wife plus the kids in addition to his job managing Woolworths. It had all kept him quite busy over the past several weeks.

"Peter" yelled a welcoming Bobby. "Come here. I was just mixing up a bourbon and water for Paul and here's one for you. Unwind and have a little fun. You need it!" He gave Peter a big pat on the back and wandered back off to the horseshoe pit.

As he was stepping up for his turn to throw the iron shoes, Bobby turned to Paul. "Hey buddy, do you think one of your sisters or their friends might be looking for a job? My secretary took off on me and I'm in it up to my eyeballs. The pay's good and we've got some great benefits. Plus, of course, there's the added benefit of working for me!"

"Oh, Bobby, my sisters don't need *those* benefits," responded Paul, "and they've already got jobs, but I'll ask Marie if she knows of anyone else."

Bobby turned and spotted Marie on the patio. "Don't bother, Paul. I see her over there. I'll ask her myself."

"How's it going, Pete?" Paul asked, as his beleaguered friend wandered over. "Are you holding up ok?"

"Well buddy, I'll tell you, I just don't know what to do about Nanette. She'll hardly eat and she's been so sick. She won't even get out of bed anymore. My sister and her husband are going to take the kids for us for a while. You know she's a teacher over in Duxbury at the Chandler School and they have plenty of room at their house. I think it will be a big help."

"Good idea Pete. That'll give her a chance to get better. Let us know if we can help. Seriously."

"Well you can help me right now by passing that bourbon," Paul said with a wry smile. "The first one went down fast."

Paul laughed, "Don't they all!"

The party did not disappoint as it went well into the night. Someone brought fireworks and, at about midnight, lit them off. That was the last straw for Ken.. He was steaming mad and hopped on the phone to the police. "This is Ken Ragaz. . ." he was quickly interrupted "Yes, Ken, we'll send someone right up the hill to you," said a stern, and slightly annoyed voice on the other end.

He went back to his late night pacing in the neighborhood. The moon was full enough to cast a glow upon the silhouettes moving about but not quite bright enough to tell every story. There were couples scattered all over the place. Some of whom had slipped off to semi-secluded places in the surrounding woods for quiet romance. But, after many drinks, they weren't so quiet. Ken saw Bobby walking down a path with someone's wife other than his own but could not make out who it was. The moonlight and the shadows were not quite cooperative enough for that. He rolled his eyes and kept on with his midnight walk.

Moments later he came across Phyllis, in her housecoat, as she was making her way back from the public beach with an arm full of not so empty alcohol bottles. She had long since left the party, but wasn't much of a sleeper in her later years and had, obviously, decided to venture out again. Talk about the nightshift, he thought.

"Phyllis! Good grief! It's after midnight! Couldn't that wait until, at least, dawn??" he exclaimed, knowing, as he spoke, that his admonitions would fall on deaf ears. Literally *and* figuratively!

"At least let me help you with those," he conceded. "It looks like you hit the jackpot tonight."

"Thank you, Ken," she replied. "Yup, it's a good haul! The beach was packed today and I expect it to be tomorrow, too. We sure got fantastic weather this Labor Day weekend. That beach really packs 'em in during the day. That's one thing I can always rely on," she said with a grin as they shuffled back toward Phyllis' house together in the moonlight.

"You're right, Phyllis," Ken grumbled. "It just gets busier and busier at that pond. Nothing like when we first moved here. The wheels of progress, right?"

"I guess, Ken, but it's good for bottle business," she grinned.

Together, they lined up the bottles on her porch. She just wouldn't wait for morning.

Ken had known her for many years and that, indeed, was one of the many things he knew.

Just then two squad cards eased up the street. The lane was barely passable with cars parked on both sides. "It's about time," Ken mumbled to himself, and he headed home.

"Colman!" yelled the crowd as he and three other officers came up the driveway. He was greeted with cheers and welcomes from the well-oiled crowd. "Well, folks, its last call. You have to start winding down the party soon," he shouted to the crowd.

Some people started to pack up and others poured one last drink for the road. Owen and Rose gathered up their things to wander back home. Paul helped a very drunk Peter to get back across the street to his front door and, before long, everyone had dispersed. Paul arrived home, from different directions, at the very same time as his wife. "Marie, honey, I barely saw you all night. Did you have a good time?"

"Yes babe. It was a fabulous night but I'm beat. Can you pay the sitter?" she said as she kissed him on the cheek. "I can't stay up another minute."

The kids were all asleep and the babysitter had her own car, for which Paul was, at that moment, very grateful. He gave her a generous tip and urged her to be extra careful driving home.

"You know, there are a lot of crazy people out there at this time of night," he reminded her. Most of them, he thought to himself, had just left the party.

Chapter 7

Digging in the Garden

With the end of summer came the end of Ken's garden. Most of what was left was starting to turn brown or was about to. He spent a few days digging up all of the remaining plants and turning over the soil for next year. He brought the last batch of tomatoes into the garage for canning and brought some extras across the street to Owen who was outside doing a little fall clean-up of his own.

"Thanks Ken. You know how Rose loves tomatoes. I see you got yourself a new tire for your truck. Just in time for the cold weather."

"Yes," Ken replied, "I'm trying to get things in order. The Farmer's Almanac says we're in for a long winter." Then, he changed the subject. "Owen, I've noticed some odd things going on around the neighborhood lately. Have you noticed anything?"

"I can't say that we have. What type of things?" asked Owen

"Let's just say there's been a lot more activity in the woods lately. I guess we've got some new, er, *nature* lovers in the area. Well, I have to be getting back to my canning. Take care."

He slowly strolled back to his garage, making sure to stop in the middle of the road, as he crossed, to eyeball each of the houses on the street for a moment or two. Then, he slowly walked back to his own house shaking his head and mumbling to no one in particular.

Later that evening, as he sat on his deck looking out over the pond, he heard someone walking in the woods just south of his house. A short while later he heard more footsteps through the woods in the darkness. Then, the muffled sounds of a man and woman's voice coming from Turtle Cove. The night's air was still, making it easy for the voices to carry back over the water. He couldn't quite make out the conversation but he knew the man's voice to be Bobby's.

About an hour later, he heard someone else making their way down the path to Turtle Cove, rummaging in the woods for a bit and then making their way back to the neighborhood just before the muffled voices drifted back up that same path.

Just then, he heard Peter's car pulling up the street. It had a very distinct sort of rumble and Ken knew it well. Peter was returning home late from work as usual as there was much work that fell to only him after the store closed in the evening. His house was dark. Nanette was in there but even Ken knew she spent most of her time sleeping these days. Peter parked and walked back up his driveway to get the family's mail. "Oh hello, Marie," he said, somewhat surprised to find her there as he reached the road.

"Peter! Hi!" she said awkwardly, as she'd not expected to greet anyone, friend or otherwise, at that hour of the night. "How was your day?"

"Same as most, I guess."

Marie was fluffing up her hair as it looked as though the day's breezes must not have been kind to her hairdo.

"Laura and I both checked on Nanette today." she said. "Laura got her to eat some more soup. That's progress."

"Thanks, Marie, for all that you both do for her. I appreciate it. But she's lost so much weight at this point and is so sick. I think we may have to get professional help for her. Her mood swings and bizarre behaviors are more concerning than anything. She'ss convinced herself that something terrible is going to happen to her and Ken will be the one doing it. She's just about out of her mind. I spoke with Dr. Isaac today and he's making arrangements for her to get a space in the hospital by next week. I haven't told her yet as I think it will only upset her more." His head hung low and it was clear in his voice that the weight of what had been was no greater than that of what was to come.

"Oh, now that's so sad Peter. Please let us all know what we can do to help." She leaned in and gave him a big hug and headed back home.

Chapter 8
She's Gone

Mid-September had arrived and ushered in a crispness to the morning air that signaled a farewell to summer. School was finally back in session, bringing with it welcome relief to parents worn down from months of summer "camp counselor" duty. Laura put her two boys on the bus, waived a cheerful goodbye as it pulled away and then hopped into her car to do the family's grocery shopping. She stopped at Nanette's house to check in on her and to see if she might need anything from the Purity Supreme supermarket in town. A short while later, she was pulling out of Nanette's driveway on her way past the pond and out of the park.

Morton Park was very quiet at this time of year. It was a dramatic difference from a month before. Not many visited the pond after Labor Day other than an occasional local resident and a few fishermen, here and there, looking for trout.

The day went by uneventfully in the neighborhood. Familiar cars and faces came and went as usual. As dusk set in, Peter Damon arrived home earlier than usual. A few moments after his arrival, the neighborhood was filled with the loud calls of Peter's worried voice calling for Nanette. He soon came barreling from his house and into the yard. Yelling and straining to see in the twilight, he was getting no response. Every house emptied into the street where a, clearly concerned, Peter was asking for any news about where he might find his wife.

"Has anyone seen her all day? Was she taken to the hospital? She was so weak.

She couldn't have gotten out of the house on her own." His voice cracked with anxiety.

Paul, who had just arrived home himself, was trying to be the calm voice of reason. "Let's check all the houses. She couldn't have gotten far in her condition. Then, we'll meet back here."

Everyone bolted back to their own homes to do their part in the search for their friend. Bobby was just pulling down the street and Laura filled him in as everyone else searched, frantically, for Nanette.

Moments dragged into what seemed to be hours for Peter but, within ten minutes, they had all collected back in the street. Peter, tears streaming from his eyes, was beside himself.

"The pond! She must've gone in the pond!" he blurted out, breathlessly, as the whole neighborhood followed him scrambling down the hill to the water's edge. Paul and Owen suggested that they call the police and the hospital just in case.

Soon the police arrived and, before long, there was an orchestrated search of the woods underway. It was, unfortunately, just getting too dark to really mount a complete and thorough search but patrolmen and neighbors alike kept walking the paths, yelling for Nanette. "Nanette, NANETTE!"

Morton Park gave up nothing that night but the echoes of their own voices across the pond.

The next morning broke with cool, dry air and, by now, the Massachusetts State Police had been called in. They came at dawn with dogs and ATVs, two dozen men and a helicopter. But their search of the woods, too, came up empty.

All eyes were, now, on the pond where a pair of State Police divers had been taking turns rolling off an inflatable boat to make their way down to the murky bottom in their best attempt at an organized grid search. Being that this is the deepest pond in Eastern Massachusetts, it proved to be an impractical search. The dark bottom closes out almost all light and its strange, swampy plant growth gives cover to almost anything that might descend from the surface.

The decision, ultimately, was made to drag the pond's bottom early that afternoon. A small barge with a dragger net was launched into the water hours later and began the methodical work of pulling its weighted net across the length of the pond's bottom, one strip at a time. Drag, hoist, inspect and dump. Turn around and repeat. It was like mowing a watery lawn. As this operation could be performed under the glow of bright floodlights, it continued well into the night until every inch of the pond's floor had been raised to the surface. Still there was nothing.

Peter was beside himself. Where could she be? The neighbors all pulled together like family to help but, soon, suspicions crept in as so often happens when trouble casts its long, dark shadow so close to home.

Detective Colman came looking for answers. He decided to split up the neighbors and interview them all separately.

It seemed he was getting the same story from everyone. Nanette was at odds with Ken. Soon, all suspicion was on the cantankerous old man. Ken was the last to be interviewed and he didn't have much to say except that he was with his old Air Corps buddy, Fred Henderson, for the day down on the Cape.

"Is Henderson gonna tell me the same story?" Coleman pressed, his eyes narrowed to slits.

"Sure thing," Ken responded without pause.

Perfect grumbled Coleman to himself as he walked back to his cruiser. Another army buddy alibi. Where's the loyalty? God, country and the law, or to the guy who dug him out of a firefight in occupied France 25 years ago. A "no-win" situation for a small town cop with no leverage. It's like no alibi at all, he thought. But try disproving it.

The search continued among neighbors and friends after the State Police cleared out. Nanette had now, officially, been missing for seven days and the investigation had no real progress to show for its effort. Each day, when the men came home from work, they would walk the woods looking for any sign of her.

It was Friday night, day seven, when Owen walked across to Ken's house where he was sitting in his garage with Fred Henderson. "Hey fellas, want to give it one more walk through the woods?"

"Sure," replied Fred, "I'll go. Come on Ken, the walk will do your old legs some good."

The three men headed south. They passed Turtle Cove and rounded the bend around to the east. Owen stopped in the path.

"You know, we've spent so much time walking around this pond that we really haven't spent much of our search through the woods over to the next couple of ponds."

"The police checked out both Lout Pond and Billington Sea Pond and all the woods around both," said Ken. "But it wouldn't hurt to check again. Let's go."

Ken and Fred had each "equipped" themselves with a pocketful, or two, of Miller High Life bottles which made the impromptu extension of their journey a more pleasant adventure despite the serious nature of their mission.

"Shhhh!" cautioned Owen softly, "I heard something. It sounds like someone talking."

Mumbled voices filtered through the trees. They appeared to be those of a man and a woman. Slowly and quietly, the men crept closer to the source of the mysterious conversation.

"Oh boy," whispered Owen, "we'd better turn back. It's Bobby and Marie!"

The three men clumsily turned and retraced their steps as fast as three old men could, actually, retrace steps in the dark. After a short while, they all stopped to catch their breath.

"Let's go back home and call the search off for the night," huffed a very out of breath Ken.

"Good idea. Do you think they saw us?" asked Owen.

Fred laughed, "Well, I'm sure they *heard* us!"

"I wish I didn't hear *them*," Owen grimaced.

They all laughed about it a little more and walked the rest of the way back home. It was the first time in a week that the tension had broken at all, among *anyone*, in Morton Park.

As the three men exited the path onto the road, they heard rustling in the wood behind them a bit.

"It must be them. Quick, into the garage!" whispered Ken as the three old timers mustered up one last hobbled sprint to the safety of his aging wooden building.

Chapter 9

Et Tu?

The weeks were passing and there was still no sign of Nanette. A certain, sad resignation began to grip those who cared. Most chose to believe that she went out for a swim, got in trouble with no one around to help, and that her body sank into one of the deep springs that fed the pond, out of reach of the dragger that had swept its bottom in vain.

Peter went on, day to day, but just seemed to wander aimlessly. He was going through the motions of life without really living any of it. His sister and brother-in-law agreed to keep the children indefinitely so that Peter could try his best to work through his loss. No one, really, had much hope for that. Especially Peter.

There was still talk around the neighborhood that Ken had something to do with Nanette's disappearance. Detective Colman would neither confirm nor deny whether Ken was a suspect. He would only state, when asked, that the investigation was still open and that no information, therefore, could be shared.

The fall air had lost all memory of summer and activity around the pond was quiet as October drew to a close. Most of the leaves were on the ground and there were reports that the first snow had already fallen up north.

The ladies finally resumed their Monday afternoon card game and Rose's friend, Betty, from North Plymouth filled in, albeit awkwardly, as their fourth.

Rose greeted Betty when she arrived. "Welcome Betty. Girls, you all know Betty."

Laura immediately took her jacket. "Welcome, Betty, to our Monday game. Can I get you a drink?"

"Whatever you are having is fine," Betty responded as she took off her muddy boots at the door. It had been a rainy autumn and the mud was starting to get the best of all of them.

"Oh Betty, before I forget," said Marie, "You and your committee did such a wonderful job again this year organizing the Holy Ghost Fair. We all had such a great time. We can hardly wait until next summer to go again. Please let me know if I can be of any help next time."

"By the way, girls, I have a new strawberry rhubarb pie recipe if anyone wants it for their Thanksgiving pie list," offered Rose as she dealt out the first hand.

"Well, I for one am not making any pies this year, or anything *else* for that matter," stated Marie. "Paul is taking the kids to his mother's here in town the night before to help out and I'm going down the Cape to Yarmouth to my parent's this year. Dad is being honored as the 'Ambassador' for the Yarmouth High School Thanksgiving Day football game. They're making a big deal over him. I think it's because he must have donated a bigger than usual check this year," she laughed. "It's amazing the accolade one's money can buy these days."

"I'll take a copy of that recipe Rose," said Laura. "Bobby loves that pie. It seems to take more and more to make that man happy lately. Marie, when are you leaving for the Cape?"

"Not 'til Thursday morning. Paul and the kids are actually sleeping at his mother's to help out Wednesday night, so I guess I get the big bed all to myself for one night." She smiled and looked away distantly.

Laura smiled as well and responded, "I'll make an extra pie for you to bring to your parents."

"Oh Marie! No cooking?" asked Betty in disbelief. "I couldn't imagine."

The game and chit chat continued for a couple of hours until, like clockwork, Rose suddenly stopped and said, "It's late. I have to get Owen's dinner. See you ladies next Monday and have a great Thanksgiving. Laura, stop by tomorrow and I'll give you that recipe." With that she was off like a lit rocket. They all said their goodbyes and wandered home to their own kitchens to create very different versions of that with which they welcomed home their men.

It was a typical Thanksgiving for all except Peter. He went to his sister's house but did not stay long. He was home early and just sat out in the cold on his back deck as he did often these days.

Paul and his kids got home late on this Thanksgiving to an empty house. He thought it odd that Marie would stay down on the Cape so late. The next morning he awoke early. His wife was still not home. She had been acting so aloof lately. Maybe she'd decided to visit with her family a while longer but, still, it was odd for her not to call. He decided he would call her parent's house after 9am just to make sure everything was ok. Something just seemed off. Why wouldn't she have called yesterday and why was there a pie uncovered on the kitchen counter? Shouldn't she have taken that with her?

When he did call, his heart skipped a beat, several, actually. Her parents thought she had changed her mind and planned to spend Thanksgiving with her husband and children. She had never arrived. Panic washed over him as the receiver slipped from his hand and dropped to the floor. "Paul? Paul? Are you there? . . ."

It was happening again . . .

Paul ran out of his house to each neighbor to report the news and to ask if they had any ideas where she could be. He was already frantic before his first stop at Peter's house. Peter had been home most of the day Thursday but did not remember seeing either Marie or her car since Wednesday evening.

"Her car was there when I went to sleep Wednesday night and not there in the morning," said Peter, a grave look of confusion and fear mirroring that of his friend. They decided to head across the street and check with the Stevens.

Before long they had spoken to everyone except Ken and Phyllis. Everyone started to gather out in the street.

"Paul, I think you should call the police," said Rose. It was determined that no one had seen her since Wednesday evening when Paul left the house.

"Laura, you must have seen her since. There is a pie you made for her on the kitchen counter that was not there when we left Wednesday," Paul said with a shaky voice.

"Well I brought the pie over around 4:30 on Wednesday. Did anyone else see her after that?" asked Laura as she looked around the crowd.

"I only saw her car there until late Wednesday night," said Peter.

Phyllis and Ken were, just then, making their way out of their respective houses and heading to the street to see what the commotion was about as Peter came running back out of his house after calling the police. He met Ken crossing his driveway.

"KEN! Do you know anything about where Marie could be? Or, my *wife*? You see everything that happens in this neighborhood. I find it hard to believe you don't know where my wife is or Marie!" he said combatively. Ken didn't reply and walked closer to the group. He looked perplexed at Owen. Owen whispered to Ken that now Marie had gone missing too. Ken's eyes widened.

Rose took Phyllis' hand and turned with her to walk back to the Anderson's house. "We will stay with the children, Paul, so they do not get alarmed. I'm sure there's a logical explanation. Let's keep our emotions in order and think clearly." Tensions were stretched to the breaking point in the neighborhood.

Paul was now confronting old man Raggazini. "Where *are* they, Ken? *TELL ME!*" He grabbed Ken's shoulders and started to shake him. The old man just stood there in shock. Owen and Bobby quickly stepped between Ken and the agitated duo of Peter and Paul. Just then two patrol cars turned the corner.

Sergeant Colman stepped out with his partner Teddy Olsen and two more officers got out of the other cruiser. "Calm down folks. It looks like things are getting a little out of hand here," instructed Colman. Paul was now getting very emotional.

"It's Ken. He knows where our wives are! He knows. I *know* he knows." A very shaken Ken took another step back and said, "The last time I saw Marie was around 10:00 pm on Wednesday night. I was driving back from the VFW and when I turned the corner she was on her front step talking with Bobby."

Laura's eyes quickly darted to Bobby who, in turn, immediately looked at Ken. "Ken you must be mistaken," Bobby snorted, defensively. "I was home in the basement playing music all night and working. Laura was upstairs cooking. She can attest to that."

"I am *not* mistaken," the old man fired back.

An enraged Bobby lunged at Ken and would have reached him had Teddy not caught him first and pulled him back. Teddy Olsen was a young guy, new to the force, and a giant of a man standing 6'4" and carrying at least 270 pounds on his frame. He had the situation easily under control.

Colman could see things were quickly spiraling out of control on Burgess Road. "Alright folks, let's all go back to your own homes and I will be by each house to speak with you all individually."

Everyone headed home. Peter went with Paul to his house and Laura walked five paces ahead of Bobby to theirs.

"Wait up Laura," Bobby said as he hastened his pace. She didn't look back and quickened her own stride. Once inside, she went to the bathroom and locked the door.

Chapter 10

Dogs Dig

Colman started at Paul's house. The children were gone. They had been invited to Phyllis' house to play. That was an exciting invitation for any kid because her house was a mini museum of junk. A "one way" museum of junk to be specific. She brought it all in and then never parted with a single thing.

Coleman had no particular need to speak to Phyllis. He was sure she had no credible information to share as she would have, undoubtedly, been asleep by early Wednesday evening. Asleep, or passed out, one or the other. Either way, an interview

with Phyllis would be a waste of time, he
was sure.

Peter and Paul were open with Colman
about their suspicions of Ken. They talked in
depth about his odd behavior over the years
and his arguments with Nanette about her
dog. They, more confidently than when it
happened, blamed him for the dog's death.
Colman had to remind them that Ken was,
surely, ruled out for the dog's demise as his
truck was not even running at the time. He'd
had no vehicle with which to have run over
the dog.

But he *was* high on Coleman's suspect list
for the women, though that sensitive
information was not shared with the agitated
men.

"Besides," Coleman counseled, "someone
accidently running over a dog wouldn't
necessarily make them a homicidal maniac,

now, would it? Peter, you take care of Paul and stay close to the phone. We're going to talk to the rest of the neighbors and then we'll be back."

The next house the police called upon was Ken's. The old man opened the door and invited them in. Not many were welcomed into Ken's house besides his buddy, Fred. As the police entered, they saw him sitting on the couch. "Fred, I didn't realize you were in town," said Colman.

"Hey, Andy. Yeah, I came up yesterday to spend the holiday with Ken. He was just filling me in on what was going on out on the street. Another one missing, that's just crazy!" he said as he sat forward and started to put on his shoes.

Colman removed his hat and sat down in a chair. "Ken, we go back a long way, but I have to let you know that fingers are pointing your way on these missing ladies. You have not kept it secret that you aren't on board with how the neighborhood has changed these past years. Do you have any insights into what might be going on?"

"Actually, Andy, I do. I see most everything that happens around here. Bobby was having an affair with Nanette before she went missing. There was a lot of distress on her part when they broke it off and then Bobby started seeing Marie."

"Whoa! Ken, those are some serious accusations. I'm not interested in rumors, just facts," said Colman.

Fred spoke up, "Andy, unfortunately it's true. I don't take Bobby as a violent man. More of a Cassanova, but I saw him coming out of Marie's on Wednesday night. I was with Ken on our way back from the VFW.

Also, a while back we were out looking for Nanette and we saw Bobby and Marie fooling around in the woods. Ask Owen. He was with us that day as well."

"Thanks for the information, fellas. If you think of anything else, give me a call. I'm going to head across the street now." He put his hat back on and turned towards the door.

"One more thing," said Ken. "When you're done with this case I've noticed a lot of items going missing from my garage. I would like to file a report before I wake up one morning to a totally empty garage."

"Teddy, stay here with Ken and make a list. I'll be across at Owen's house." Then he turned and left.

"Owen, Rose, may I come in?"

"Of course, Andy. Come right in. May I get you some coffee and pie?" asked Rose.

"Yes, thank you, that sounds great! We were just across the street at Ken's and he tells me, Owen, that you witnessed Marie and Bobby, together, recently."

"Yes, Colman, I'm sad to say that's true. Living here, at the end of the street, we see a lot of things that go on in the woods. Up until now we've kept to ourselves and thought it wasn't for us to judge, but we have to tell you that we've seen Bobby going in and out of these woods this past year with Nanette, Marie and other ladies from their parties. We don't think his wife knows the extent of it but we have to believe she has an idea."

Rose took Owen's hand and added, "But we try not to gossip and we *definitely* do not think Bobby is violent. Today, in the street, was the first time we saw him lose his temper when Ken exposed him for his indiscretions in front of his wife."

Moments later, patrolman Olsen came to the door. "We found her car. It's down the street at the Cadillac Motel," he said quietly to Coleman.

"Oh geez, don't tell her husband," groaned Colman. "Thank you folks," he said, as he turned his attention back to Owen and Rose. "I've got to go. And, thanks for the pie, Rose."

The Callahans walked the policemen to the door and out to the front porch. As the officers were heading down the driveway, Rose saw her black Labrador, Gibby, coming out of the woods.

"What in the world does that dog have?" she exclaimed. Owen turned to look.

"MY GOD! Rose go in the house right now!" He practically pushed her through the front door, closed it and started for the dog.

"Andy!" he hollered as he rushed down the steps toward his Labrador. The officers came hustling back up the driveway. As they got closer to Owen, they could see what he saw. Gibby was dragging a human leg out of the woods.

Chapter 11

The Other Pond

Coleman had the street locked down with no one coming in or out of the neighborhood. He'd called in the State Police who arrived within the hour with their cadaver dogs.

The leg the dog found could not have been Marie's as it was in a state of advanced decomposition that could not, possibly, have occurred in less than 36 hours. The Plymouth policeman also believed it could not be Nanette's as he knew she was last seen with bright red nail polish on her hands and feet. Always the glamour girl but, now, the vanished girl, he thought. Something dramatic was hovering over this little neighborhood and it was threatening to poison the whole town for a very long time.

The State Police brought their specially trained dogs. They started in the woods around Little Pond and walked the same paths as they had when they searched for Nanette originally. The dogs and their handlers searched for hours into the afternoon, with no luck. Then, Colman had an idea. He went to Owen and asked him if he would be willing unleash Gibby and let him out to run free. Owen agreed, opened the door, and Gibby took off. She headed for the woods with the team of officers struggling to keep up. Gibby ran around to the south side of the pond and then through the woods to Billington Sea Pond. Teddy was the only one fit enough, and young enough, to keep up with the dog and even *he* was getting winded. Finally, Gibby stopped at the edge of the neighboring pond, panting almost as heavily as Officer Olsen. The rest of the officers, ultimately, stumbled out of the wood to the water's clearing like the last few, out of shape, runners in a marathon that they never should have entered.

They all stood there frozen, looking in disbelief at the partially dug up body of a girl that had been exposed by the dog. It was something none had ever seen before and, all hoped to never see again. All of them felt faint, some turned away to be sick and a few welled up with tears. Not that there wasn't reason for *all* of them to do so.

The careful excavation began. Over the rest of the day and into the evening, they dug. When it got dark and cold, they set up lights and a built small fire to warm the men. Most were in a state of shock and did not notice the 22 degree evening. All in all, they uncovered three bodies. One newly buried, and known to be Marie, one believed to be Nanette and a third, unidentified, young woman.

Back on Burgess Road, the air was heavy with grief. The news crews had now descended upon the neighborhood and the police were doing their best to shield the families. Peter and Paul were inconsolable. Owen and Rose stayed with them and tried to care for them both.

Several policemen, led by Colman, walked up the Stevens' driveway and knocked.

"Robert Stevens, you will have to come with us. You are under arrest for murder."

"Wait! What? Me? What do you mean? I had nothing to do with this!" he declared frantically as they led him to a patrol car.

The squad car passed the main beach on its way out. There, the news photographers' cameras were flashing and popping in the dark as they took up the chase to the police station.

Colman stayed behind to speak with Laura. "Laura, do you understand what has been happening here?" he asked as tenderly as he could.

"Yes, I think so," she stuttered, shaken to the point where she needed to brace herself against the wall just to remain standing. "I heard there is a third girl. I think it might be his former secretary. I, I . . just don't know what to think anymore." Her words trailed off as she slid, slowly, down the wall and collapsed onto the floor in the hallway where tears finally began to flow. "What will happen to Bobby?" she sobbed.

"I'm not sure. We've arrested him tonight and he'll be arraigned on Monday morning. I doubt he will get a bail opportunity and we'll have to see what happens at the trial. You need to make arrangements for yourself now, Laura, and for your children," Coleman said gently. "Take all the help that people offer. Let us know if you need anything." He said said goodbye and left. As he was backing his cruiser out, Phyllis came up the driveway. She moved impressively well for a woman who had already celebrated 90 years of life.

"Oh dear, dear Laura, let me help you with the children. You've been through so much, you poor thing. You go and rest and Auntie Phyllis will take these sweet kids to stay and play over at my house with the Anderson kids. C'mon kids, let get some toys and clothes."

"Thank you Phyllis. I need to sort things out. This will be a great help. Bring them back in the morning and we'll all have breakfast together here," Laura said struggling to compose herself in front of the kids.

After Phyllis left with the children, Laura sat at her kitchen table looking out the back window, as she often did, into the darkness of the night. She stayed there all night until the day broke.

That night, no doubt, not a person on Burgess Road slept more than a wink but, by dawn, most had nodded off for a moment or two. The neighborhood rallied around Peter, Paul and Laura. Everyone pitched in with the kids and helped Peter and Paul to plan the two funeral services. They all learned, days later, that the third body was, indeed, that of Bobby's missing young secretary. Another tragic loss.

On Saturday morning, Phyllis brought the clan of kids over to Laura's house. Laura wanted to do all of the cooking for breakfast as she said it would keep her mind busy. Phyllis played in the living room with the children. She was running out of ideas for games and decided to play another round of hide the G. I. Joe doll. Laura finished up the two plates she'd made up for Paul and Peter and ran them across the street.

The kids were all hiding their eyes (or were supposed to be) in the kitchen as Phyllis tried to find another place to hide that darn doll. The fireplace! That was a good spot. As she bent down and moved the anvil, she noticed a loose stone. She pulled it back and tried to slip the doll in the hole but something was blocking the way. She pulled the doll back out and reached in. Out came a small can. A can of rat poison. What a funny place to keep this, she thought. And, what a terrible risk that the kids might get into it. She stood up with the ash covered can in her hand just as Laura came back in the front door. As she turned around, their eyes met.

"Laura, do you think Bobby might have poisoned them?"

Laura quickly ran to Phyllis and grabbed the can out of her hand. "Phyllis what were you doing in the fireplace? I'll take that. Actually, Phyllis, you might be right. I'll give this to the police myself. You know, you've been such a great help with the kids and now finding this . . . let me give you something for your troubles. You really should go home and rest now. I'm fine with the kids."

She reached behind the bar and grabbed a big unopened bottle of Jack Daniels. "Here, you've been such a dear. Now you go home and rest. I know all those boys must have exhausted you."

Breakfast had been all but forgotten.

"Oh Laura, thank you so very much," cooed Phyllis warmly. "You shouldn't have but since you did, I'll be on my way." Phyllis was beaming with a smile that made her almost look young. On her way out she turned back to Laura, "Oh sweetie, do you have any Coca Cola by chance?"

"Yes, Phyllis, here take this bottle. It's full and should be just enough to compliment the JD. Thanks again."

Laura ushered Phyllis out the door and quickly ran the poison down to her bedroom.

"Hey where's G I Joe?" hollered a little voice from the kitchen. "That crazy old lady must have taken him home. She's lonely," said another.

Oh, the kids, Laura remembered, and breakfast!

Chapter 12

Detective Ken

It was the Saturday night of a very eventful holiday weekend in the woods. Ken still had his house guest, Fred. They talked endlessly of the recent events and of the different scenarios that could explain what might have happened. Ken felt very unsettled about things.

It was late, around 11:00 pm, when Ken decided to go out to his garage to turn out the lights and close it up for the night. He had become especially diligent about this since his possessions had begun "walking out" of the building. Fred accompanied him with a different motivation entirely. There were more frosty Millers High Life's out there. As the men approached the garage, they heard the slap of a screen door closing hard from the direction of the Stevens' house and footsteps going down the driveway, then, turning up the street away from them toward Phyllis' house. It was a moonless night on the street and they were, therefore, left to rely on their auditory senses alone. Not enough to satisfy either of them and, given the dramatic events of the last several days, they chose to investigate. Slowly, and quietly, they made their way to the other end of the street but all was quiet now. Then, they heard a twig break in Phyllis' yard behind her house. It wasn't much but it wasn't natural either. They quietly crept up her driveway in time to see a figure just slipping inside through the back kitchen window.

They crouched low and snuck around to the front of the house where there was a big picture window. From there they could see a figure inside the house moving around the kitchen. Then, suddenly, the light came as the refrigerator door opened and they saw Laura with something in her hand. She was pouring something into a Coca Cola bottle that she had removed from the refrigerator. As she turned to put the bottle back in the fridge, Fred could see the object in her other hand. It was a small canister that had a piece of yellow tape wrapped around it with three X's marked on it.

"Hey, Ken, don't you mark all your poison containers with yellow tape and triple X's? Are you missing a can of rat poison?!"

"Aw crap, let's stop this, Fred!" Ken ran to the back door with his war buddy close behind and, together, they crashed through into the kitchen shocking Laura to the point where she could move neither her feet, nor her tongue.

"Stay right there, little lady. We saw what you did and we're calling the cops," Ken said as Fred dialed the kitchen phone. Laura's frozen limbs were instantly thawed by a rush of adrenalin and she reacted. Opening the can, she threw the poison at Ken's eyes. His glasses blocked most of the powder but he quickly dove to the sink to rinse out the rest. Fred dropped the phone, just as he had dialed the police, and tackled Laura to the ground. As he got her restrained, he scrambled back over to the phone to respond to the queries of a very curious, and concerned, dispatcher.

Coleman and his partner soon arrived, this time with flashing lights and wailing sirens heralding their arrival. After a brief and breathless discussion, Laura was handcuffed and placed in the back of a squad car.

A husband and wife, both in handcuffs within 24 hours of each other, Coleman noted. This was absolutely crazy!

Ken's eyes were clearing as the two men walked outside to give more formal statements. When they had told their story, Ken realized no one had even bothered to check on Phyllis. She had slept through all the noise and chaos. Accompanied by Coleman, they went back inside and woke her up. After telling her the story of seeing Laura attempting to poison her soda bottle, she connected a few more dots for Coleman with her own story of finding the poison in Laura's chimney and her strange behavior once it had been discovered. When she had exhausted her memory, and answered all of Coleman's questions, she made one final statement. "Boy, I sure need a drink!" They all laughed.

"I think we all could use one," said Ken.

What no one in the group but Coleman knew, as they walked out of Phyllis' house that night, was that, at least, one of the autopsy reports had returned with a finding of something called Diphacinone in the bloodstream. The compound, commonly known to anyone with a few years of high school chemistry under their belt, was an active ingredient in, among other things, rat poison.

"What a mess," he said, under his breath, to no one in particular.

Chapter 13

Police Headquarters

Colman walked into the interrogation room and found Laura pacing back and forth. She was disheveled and a bit frantic. She asked for a cigarette but she was only half done with the one she was holding.

"Laura, do you think we can talk now?" he asked. "I want to ask you about your friends."

"My friends?! My *friends*?! First of all Andy, Carol was not my friend. She was a little tramp messing around with my husband."

"Well ok then, let's start with the little tramp messing around with your husband, shall we?"

"She thought I was so dumb," Laura groused. "Well, I showed her, don't ya think? She kept calling the house for him. Day after day! One day I decided to have the call reversed and it went straight back to the Cadillac Motel. Right down the street. I couldn't believe that Bobby was bringing that little tramp right into our town. I just couldn't believe it! So I went over there to confront her. I didn't mean for things to go as far as they did."

"Laura, before you say anything else, it's my duty to ask you if you would like an attorney," Coleman said.

"Oh, Andy, there's no lawyer that can help me at this point," Laura whispered with an aire of darkness about her.

"Well then, let's keep talking," he said, "what happened at the Cadillac Motel?"

"I arrived, found her car in front of Room 3b, and knocked on the door. You can imagine her surprise when she answered it and saw me. I pushed my way right through that little tramp and the next thing I know we're rolling around on the floor. We banged into the table, I think, and a lamp fell off. I grabbed it and hit her over the head. In my rage I just kept hitting her over and over again until she stopped moving. I didn't know whether she would wake up again or not but figured I had to get her out of there before somebody else, probably Bobby, came looking for her. That bastard!"

"So I just got up, fixed myself a bit in the bathroom, and then we left," Laura said, as plainly as if she was telling a story to a friend.

She told Coleman of how she had dragged
the body into the trunk of the "little tramp's"
car and drove it to Billington Sea Pond
where no one ever goes after Labor Day.

"I left her in the trunk for the night and
snuck home through the woods. When I got
back home, no one had even noticed I was
gone."

"The next night, I went back. I just had to
see. I wasn't really even sure she was dead
but I brought a shovel just in case. Either to
hit her with, or bury her with," she said with
a little chuckle that made her almost
unrecognizable, Coleman thought.

"It took me a while but I dug a hole near the
water's edge where the ground was still soft
and I buried her. But you know that, for
God's sake. You *found* her!"

Then she drove the car around to the high
embankment on the other side of the pond

and let it roll down the hill into the water. "It just sunk, almost without a sound," she said, somewhat wistfully.

"I was so angry with Bobby at that point. I blamed him for putting me in the situation to have done what I did. I was down in Ken's garage putting the shovel back and saw the rat poison. I brought it back to my house, with every intention of poisoning the cheating bastard. And I tried! Every time I had a drink or a plate of food ready for him, he suddenly had to run out with one excuse after another. I decided to follow him one evening and that's how I found out he was having an affair with Nanette. My so-called *friend*." Coleman could see she was shaking with the rage that the memories of that discovery still re-awakened.

Laura stopped talking, put out her cigarette and lit up a new one. She paused, took a long drag and blew out the smoke slowly.

"Oh, dear Nanette. Now, that was a double disappointment. They *both* betrayed me. She was always such a flirt so, at first, I didn't think anything of it. But, over time, I knew."

"Oh, and by the way, that little dog? Let's just say it couldn't outrun my Buick," she said defiantly.

"Then, on that day of her little Tuppy's *oh so tragic* demise, I heard the two of them in the street. He broke it off with her right there in her driveway that night," she pronounced, as if it had been *her* victory.

"She was pretending to be so cut up about losing her dog but I knew what was really going on. The more depressed she got over that damned dog, and the more pity everyone showered upon her just made me sick. So I made *her* sick. I slowly gave her that poison. I really only intended to make her sick for a while but then, one day, I guess it got the best of her. I never realized that it would make her seem crazy too. That was an added bonus," she smiled.

"I went over to check on her one morning and she was just lying there . . dead. I couldn't let anyone find out about the poison so I had to do something. That morning I wrapped her in a sheet, dragged her to my car and rolled her into the trunk. Later that night I drove her over to keep that little tramp, Carol, company."

She walked over to the window and looked out over Russell Street. "I don't know what the big problem is with the neighbors around here and these bars on the window. You'd think it would make them feel safer. This would have been a much better neighborhood for us to have settled in, I think," she mused as she turned back around to Colman.

He looked up from his notepad, "I'd have to agree with you there. Laura, what about Marie?"

"Ah, yes, Marie. She was worse than the others because I never saw that coming. She had a great husband at home. What in the world would she want with *Bobby*? She really had me believing she was my friend but I suppose if she could betray her sweet husband then it couldn't have been that difficult to betray me as well. Bobby must have used his slippery silver tongue on her too," she grumbled, as her face grew dark.

"Honestly, I was shocked, after Nanette went missing, at the audacity of those two to start up like they did. I paid her a visit to drop off the pie right before Bobby got home that Wednesday afternoon. Dinner was brief at our house that night and Bobby insisted on going downstairs to listen to his records and to, *supposedly*, work on an important ad campaign. He told me not to disturb him so I sent the kids to bed early and stayed in the kitchen baking and preparing the meal for the following day. But, as I was at the kitchen sink, I saw him sneak out of the bulkhead stairway. I ran down to the bedroom window and saw him go into Marie's house. I knew Paul and the kids were already gone."

Laura stopped talking and sat down. She just sat and stared for a while. Then she put out her cigarette and leaned across the table. She looked straight into Colman's face.

"Do you have any idea what it's like to be betrayed? To try harder and harder only to find yourself further behind than where you started?"

"So, I waited until Bobby was back and everyone was asleep. Then I snuck over to her house and let myself in. You know she never locked her doors," she mused.

"She was sound asleep. I had taken one of Bobby's ties and, as she woke, I wrapped it around her neck. It took a while and she struggled but eventually she went to, you know, sleep. I dragged her out to her own car and drove her to Billington Sea Pond too. Then I brought her car over to the Cadillac Motel and left it there so her husband could see what a cheating whore she really was and so Bobby, the *bastard*, could see that she'd been found out. It made me so sick to see her husband idolize her and treat her so well and all the while she was deceiving him. She made a fool out of him just as much as she did me."

"Didn't you think it was wrong?" Coleman asked. "Didn't you imagine you would get caught?"

Laura got up, wandered back to the window and stared for a while. "I knew I would but, honestly Andy, the prison I've been in for so long has been so much worse than the one I'm trading it for. I actually feel free," she said breezily.

Colman got up and collected his papers. She turned back to look at him again, "Colman, do you want to know the worst part?"

"I didn't think it *could* get much worse but, ok, what is it?"

"It was all like a dream. I guess you wouldn't understand. I guess I don't even really get it. It was like a movie and I was watching the entire thing and couldn't stop any of it."

She lit up another cigarette and turned her gaze back through the bars to the activity on the other side of the window. He shook his head and looked at her one last time.

"Maybe someday you'll see how your selfish and vicious acts hurt so many more than just your victims."

Then he closed and locked the door.

Several days later, Bobby was released from the Plymouth County Jail. He went back to the neighborhood to pick up his kids from the Callahan's house where Owen and Rose, along with others in the Burgess Road neighborhood, had been caring for them.

"Listen guys," he said to those who had come out to greet him, "I am really so sorry about everything. C'mon kids, say goodbye to your friends. We are going to move in with Grandma and Grandpa for a while."

Bobby took the kids, went home and packed what he could fit it the family car and then no one ever saw them again. Days later, a moving van backed into the driveway and a For Sale sign went up in the yard.

Paul and Peter didn't have much to say to Bobby that day when he returned for his kids. They were, understandably, still reeling from the impact their former friend had visited upon their lives. But, after he left, Paul turned to Peter and said "I suppose we should head over to Ken's. I'm sure we all owe him an apology."

Months later, at her trial, Laura was deemed insane and sentenced to life in the Taunton State Mental Hospital. She died in July of '78 after yet, another, unsuccessful experimental "therapy" session.

Things in Morton Park went back to normal after a while. The Stevens house was sold and the new owner, none other than Ken's buddy Fred, fit in nicely with the other neighbors. That especially made old man Raggazini happy.

Peter remarried a great gal he met from Woolworths and they went on to have two more kids. Paul never remarried but enjoyed his children and, eventually, grandchildren living the same simple life in the same sweet spot on Little Pond.

Owen and Rose drifted back into own their routine and, of course, the wonderfully fabulous Phyllis continued her great work saving the beach from all the partially consumed bottles of "litter."

58878455R00075

Made in the USA
Columbia, SC
28 May 2019